BLACK IRISH

BY

C.S ANDERSON

C. S Anderson

ALUCARD PRESS

CHAPTER ONE

More proof, if some were needed, that God hates me. I am in an Irish styled pub on Friday the thirteenth in one of the most boring suburbs of Seattle. It's nine thirty seven and a pretty young woman is playing the guitar and working her way through a Van Morrison tune.

If Van Morrison was dead, he would be spinning in his grave.

If Van Morrison was undead, he would have been ripping the untalented bitch's throat out.

Still, I'm not here for the entertainment, I am a man on a mission and the pint in front of me or the girl singing is not part of that mission. I am here to meet someone and that someone is late, never a good sign in my line of work. They are bringing me something that I need to do what I do and the fact that they are late is

2

raising the hairs on my neck more than I am particularly comfortable with. Aside from that there are two Renfields in the bar with me.

The Renfields so far have not noticed me, it works that way sometimes. I am lying as low as a six foot six bald black guy who tips the scales at almost three hundred pounds can do.

Especially in a suburban Irish bar.

I hate Renfields. I hate them in a way that nobody but one of us could ever possibly understand.

I hate Renfields because I used to be one of them.

Now I am a Gun.

Joe Gunn is what people call me, when they call me anything. My other name is only spoken by those whom I hunt.

They call me, Black Irish.

The scars on my left arm burn to let me know that the Renfields are there. Not so very coincidently there are thirteen of the marks.

One for each victim I served up to the vampire that used to be my master. More accurately nine of them burn, four of them have faded and gone quiet as I avenged the deaths of my race that I have caused.

When all of the scars go dark and quiet I will die and face whatever eternal punishment faces me.

I hunger for that day. In a way that you will never understand.

Vampire hunting has its jargon, its lingo just like any subculture does. If you make quilts you know what the hell mitered corners are even though it might baffle the fuck out of me. I am, what is called, a Gun, someone trained to take out vamps. Renfields are slaves that find victims for their vampire masters. We have a loosely organized group of helpers called Widows, whether they are male or female, tradition dictates that they are called Widows. It comes from the fact that most of them have lost a loved one to vampires and seek to aid in their destruction.

The Widow comes through the front door, I make her at once. Short, mousy brown hair but curvy and attractive dressed in black from head to toe. Her eyes cast about for a moment or two and then fix on my own. I blink her the code and she blinks the proper response back to me.

So I don't blow her head off.

Instead I nod and wave for her to join me at my booth. She approaches warily and I give her good marks for that. Far too many Widows end up dead because at some level they thought that working for a Holy cause guarded you from evil. It didn't, in fact a good rule of thumb in the survival game was...

The Good Lord helps those who help themselves.

For that reason my 9mm Hi Point Model C is in the hand she can't see under the table. I used to carry a Glock, but it failed me once, so I retired it. Now, I buy American. My Hi Point reminds me of me, cheap, big, black, ugly and utterly reliable to do what it is designed to do.

I trust nobody any more than I trust myself.

She is all business, no small talk. Looking me in the eye she hands me a small package under the table.

I take it and it has the right weight. One hundred rounds of ammo blessed by a priest, secretly of course for those I work for do not officially exist. I have been a busy boy lately and I have not had time to visit our weapons guy between killing vamps and Renfields and any other piece of crap that is foolish enough to get in the way of what I need to do. So I put out the call with a coded internet message and lo and behold a Widow shows up with what I require.

A sour taste fills my mouth and my scars begin to burn. This can only mean one thing.

There is a vampire right outside of the bar.

Cursing, I stash the ammo and hiss at the Widow to bail out the back door of the bar. As she walks away I recite the spell my trainer literally beat into me. It is in a language that predates Latin and I have no idea what it means, but in theory it blanks her for a few minutes to vampire perception, so that she has an honest chance of escaping alive.

It is the least I can do.

There is a flicker of movement on the very edges of my perception and the vamp is sitting across from me. She is tiny, barely five feet with green eyes, red hair and delicate features. Her arrival was so sudden and smooth that the singer on the stage never missed a beat. My training tells me that she is not quite an elder, she might be a hundred or so, but no more than that. She can still, with some effort at glamour, pass for human.

"Oh, you have been so very, very naughty." She tells me in a playful breathless voice.

She must want something, she is fast enough to tear my throat out before I can aim my gun at her head and fire. We both know it. I put my gun on the table between us and put my hand palms down on the table. The only fatal vamp kill shot me and my blessed bullets can count as a down and out win is, multiple head shots.

Anything else on a vamp this age will just piss them off.

"One does ones best." I give her my most charming smile, it works well on human women, but vamps could generally care less. Still, force of habit and all that.

The Renfields in the bar are reacting to her presence now, they begin to approach groveling in their need to serve. They make me sick, more so because not so very long ago I was one of them. That knowledge both angers and sickens me. She dismisses them with a sharp wave of her pale hand and just like that, they are gone.

"Such a bad boy you are. My master wishes to speak with you." She sounds bored, but I can hear tones in her voice that suggest otherwise.

I was going to put together some witty reply, but before I had the chance, the Widow I masked with my spell comes back in and sprays the vamp in the face with a mace unit modified to spray Holy water and silver nitrate. The vamps hands flutter to her ruined face like startled birds and she starts screaming, hell I would scream too if my face was melting. The bar erupts into chaos and the Renfields come running at me. Snarling, I snatch my pistol off of the table and kill both Renfields as they come charging back into the bar. A bouncer comes running at me and without even thinking I backhand him away. I follow the Widow out the back door to my Harley and in a few seconds we are gone daddy, gone.

One vamp maimed and two Renfields dead, things could have gone a hell of a lot worse. Except, behind me now on my bike was a Widow who had just messed up a hundred year old vamp and was a random factor in whatever game was now afoot. First order of business was to get some answers from her, she was no normal Widow, they did not carry such weapons and did not pull stunts like what just happened.

Her breasts were crushed against my back, and me being me that was beginning to get to me. Hell, my lack of ability to keep it in my pants was what led me into this life and even in this long shot chance at redemption, I was still prone to thinking with my other head.

"Don't get happy big boy, I took a vow of celibacy." She shouts into my ear as we get the hell out of Dodge.

Have I mentioned that God hates me?

CHAPTER TWO

We park the Harley in an alley behind a warehouse in Pioneer Square, as we walk away from it I mutter a simple masking spell and the bike becomes all but invisible in the shadows. I took the work of beauty off of a Renfield I killed a couple of months ago and just haven't found the time to turn it over to The Order like I am supposed to. I love the thing and want to keep it and thus far I have operated by the forgiveness is easier to get than permission mode of operation.

I do that a lot.

Come on, it is a custom stretched and molded frame with Mackey Heads and .600 lift cam and a flat black custom paint job with eighty spoke Akront wire wheels. It is all beautiful chrome and midnight dark blackness and I love this machine.

Procedure be damned.

My scars are silent, so for the moment we are safe, relatively speaking of course. No vamps or Renfields in the immediate area anyway. The Widow stands looking at me with a, "What now?" look on her face.

"Thanks for the assistance. You can call me Joe. What's your name?"

"You can call me Keela. We left a pretty big mess back there in the bar." Her tone is even but I, due to my training, can hear notes of stress and adrenaline in her voice. Whoever she is, she is still basically a civilian, not a professional.

"The Order will clean it up and spin doctor the news. Just another bout of gang related violence. Why did you come back? The idea was for you to get away clean."

She didn't answer for a long moment and when she did she was looking away from me, off into the night.

"I hate them."

"Fair enough. The Order has a safe house apartment in this warehouse. We should lie low until dawn and then try to figure out what's what. The vamp you sprayed said that her master wanted to talk to me and that fails to give me a warm fuzzy feeling."

Without waiting to see if she will follow me or not I turn and start walking towards the warehouse. I have questions for her, but I don't want to ask them standing in a dark alley after severely pissing off the local vamp community. My questions can wait until we are securely behind a very locked and warded door.

She follows me into the warehouse and I notice that she doesn't shiver as she passes the protective wards that guard the doorways. I do because of the vampire taint in my blood, the taint on my soul. I can feel the wards for the same reason that there are small burns on my skin where a drop or two of the Holy water hit me when she maced the vamp in the bar, because I am not quite human anymore.

Keela apparently is. She passes through the second ward guarding the door to the apartment without reacting and we are in. The place is spartan at best, a couple of couches, a postage stamp size kitchenette and an equally small bathroom. No hanging pictures, no personal touches of any kind. I say a small prayer and open the refrigerator.

Low and behold there is beer. Maybe God has hated me enough for one night. I grab one and plop down onto one of the couches and turn my full undivided attention on my guest.

"Talk to me. You aren't any kind of Widow I have ever come across, who gave you that vamp mace? Who the hell are you?"

She just got me out of a tight spot so, I would hate like hell to shoot her but my hand rests lightly on my gun. If she goes for the mace in her bag or any other kind of weapon I will do what I have to do. That information is apparently in my voice because she doesn't bother lying or refusing to answer.

"Not very long ago I was a nun. Then I lost my brother and mother to a vampire attack. I… lost my faith and left my order. A priest contacted me about becoming a Widow, screw that, I wanted to kill the damn things. He put his hands on me and told me that women weren't fit for the task. I asked him if he was trying to get into my pants." Her voice is devoid of emotion, she might as well be reciting a grocery list.

"The whole celibacy vow thing?" I asked as gently as I could.

"I told him that he had zero chance of getting in my pants for the simple reason that one asshole in there was enough. Then I broke his nose and stole the mace. He slunk back to The Order and approved me to be a Widow."

My training has turned me into what amounts to a human lie detector machine, I interpret tone of voice and body language and a thousand and one other tell tales and I know the truth when I hear it.

That being said I also know that there are a lot of things that she isn't telling me.

We sat silently for a while, each lost in our own thoughts. The lady had spunk but without training spunk just got you killed. I had no idea what to do with this one, the vamp she had maimed would be literally out for blood tomorrow night. The issue of why her master had wanted me still was unresolved as well.

"There is sandwich stuff in the fridge, pick a couch and get some sleep. You did well tonight. Tomorrow we will have to make some moves." I drained my beer and settled down on the couch I was lying on.

She gave me a long studied glance and then shrugged and nodded ok to the arrangement. I was asleep before she was, right up to the point where I nodded off I could feel the weight of her stare. I had been up for days and the need for sleep slaps me upside the head and drags me under.

To the usual nightmares that await me.

It always starts the same, me in a bar up on Capitol Hill spreading the charm around looking for a girl to warm my bed that night. That was me that was what I was all about. The blonde with green eyes seemed random to me at the time, maybe like the movements of lions might seem random to gazelles. I thought that I had picked her out of the pack, but it turns out she had been hunting me.

Thing was, she was never the real threat. She told me her name was Jasmine and that she was a dental hygienist. I didn't ask for a whole lot of other details. She was beautiful and seemed into me. We ended up back at her place.

She was a Renfield.

Her master came into the bedroom as Jasmine was riding me and as casually as you or I might swat a fly she pulled the girl off of me, broke her neck, tossed her to the far side of the room and took her place. All in one horrible blink of the eye. As she rode me, she took a nip on my wrist and drank from me.

Then she nipped her wrists and shoved it against my mouth. I drank from her.

I became her slave that night.

Never found out why she killed her Renfield and replaced her with me. The older the vamps get the more alien and captious they become, their thoughts and motivations becoming completely unknowable to us humans. Maybe a complete whim, maybe part of some larger plan, I will never know.

Once a month or so, from then on, I would go out and seduce a victim back to where my master waited to feed. They died each and every single one of them. I felt no guilt, no remorse. My every waking thought centered on pleasing and serving my new master. My reward was each day she placed one drop of her blood on my eager tongue.

The dream then marches me through that time in my life and shows me the faces of each and every human I served up to my master's hunger.

As always, I wake up in a cold sweat swallowing a scream.

And as usual, I wake up to bigger problems.

My scars burn hot. Renfields have found us, a whole lot of them apparently. All right outside the building, so far none of them have braved the wards just yet.

"Rise and shine lady, we got trouble." I tell her as I get to me feet and draw my gun.

To her credit she is on her feet next to me in a heartbeat. Her hands shake slightly, but she is holding her mace at the ready.

"It is past dawn, so it can't be vamps right?" She asks me in a low voice.

I nod. In the real world vampires don't fucking sparkle in sun light. They burst into flames and burn to ash. Newbies burn up quickly, but even the most ancient of elders cannot survive the light of day.

"Renfields. Lots of them, don't know how they tracked us or whose they are, but they are out there. If I give you a gun can you use it? I mean that a couple of ways Sunshine, one, do you know how and two, can you kill something that looks human? I know you hate vamps enough, but will you kill Renfields?"

"I have never fired a gun, but I am a quick study and I have no problem with killing them. A Renfield lured my brother and mother to their deaths." Her voice holds a lot of emotions we don't have time to sort out just now.

I rip the cushions from the couch I had been sleeping on, beneath them is a large box containing a few back up weapons. Looking over what's available I pick up a Ruger LCP 9mm. I rack the slide and hand it to her.

"Safety is off. Just point and shoot. You have seven rounds, if that isn't enough to get us to the bike, we are screwed anyway. Go for head shots, Renfields are tougher than normal humans and can take more damage. I would take it as a personal favor if you could avoid shooting me, by the way."

She gives me a ghost of a smile and holds the weapon pointing down at the floor.

"I will do my best."

A shiver runs down my spine as I feel the first ward fail. I rack a round into my gun and hold a finger to my lips to warn her to be silent. I have no idea how the bastards found us. Safe houses are supposed to be, well safe. Things are happening fast and weird but now is not the time to play detective.

Now is the time to play assassin.

Someone, or maybe more accurately something begins knocking softly but insistently at the apartment door.

We exchange a look and she nods at me to make my best judgment call. I shrug and walk over to the door.

Whatever is on the other side must sense me somehow because a high pitched voice that sounds that cotton candy soaked in blood comes warbling through the door.

"Little pigs, little pigs, let me come in."

I sigh, I hate playing games. Shoot at me or don't shoot at me. Kill me or leave me the fuck alone. Vampires and Renfields love games and drama and it just pisses me the hell off.

"Not by the hair of my chinny chin chin motherfucker." I yell and then I empty a clip through the door. I push the magazine eject and before the magazine hits the floor I have reloaded.

There is a long silent pause. The air smells like gunpowder and our ears are ringing from eight hollow points ripping through the door.

"Then I will huff and I will puff and I will blow the door in." The sick giggly voice tells us.

Using the enhanced speed I have through my vampire taint I grab the girl, flip the couch over and throw us both down behind it. I cover my ears and she is smart enough to copy me and do the same.

The door blows inward and lands back somewhere near the kitchenette. I shoot the first idiot through the door and Keela nails the second and third. The first one she killed falls and sends a revolver sliding our way and I pick it up and kill the fourth and fifth with it. It is too easy, these guys are just cannon fodder meant to soften us up for whatever is to come.

This is insane, no one vampire has this many Renfields to throw away and vampires really don't tend to work together all that well. Added to the safe house they shouldn't have been able to find and none of this makes sense.

A master vampire sent a hundred year old vamp to try and bring me in for a discussion. There were over a dozen master vamps in the state so that in and of itself told me nothing. Since becoming a Gun I had killed four vampires and countless Renfields and other assorted dirt bags, maybe I had pissed someone off.

I tended to have that effect on those around me.

"Oh this simply will not do. Before the local boys in blue come to investigate all this horrible noise, might I just step in for a word with you?" The same sickly sweet voice pipes up from out in the smoke filled hallway.

Screw it, I needed answers and whatever was out there was right. We had made a lot of noise and even in this neighborhood, officer friendly would be along sooner or later. I was in no mood to try to explain myself to them.

"Come in slow with your hand where I can see them. We can talk and then I will still probably end up shooting you." I called out. Keela looks at me like I am insane.

I am in no mood to try and explain myself to her either.

This earns me another sick giggle, the sound grates on me and makes me feel somehow unclean for the hearing of it.

A human servant steps through the door.

They are very rare things. When a Renfield has especially pleased its master, sometimes the master decides to reward them. Most Renfields are kept on a starvation diet of a drop of blood at a time, but the process of creating a human servant involves much more vamp blood and the services of one adept at dark magic. Very old, very powerful master vampires create them to have a formidable servant to do their bidding during the day light hours they themselves cannot exist in. They aren't the desperate cringing slaves that Renfields are. They are intelligent, resourceful, ruthless and utterly loyal to their masters.

They are also very very hard to kill. In some ways even harder than vamps themselves. They live as long as their masters do without aging at all. They are far stronger and faster than a normal human.

Or even a trained Gun such as myself.

This one is a razor thin white man who looks about forty or so. He is immaculately dressed in a charcoal grey suit that costs about a hundred times as much as my entire wardrobe does. He has hair so blonde that it is almost colorless and washed out pale blue eyes. His smile is just ever so slightly mocking as he steps into the room, careful not to get any blood on his expensive looking shoes.

I can almost smell the evil coming off of him

Keela shoots at him before I can warn her.

He makes a dismissive hiss through thin moist lips and a slight flicking gesture with his left hand. The bullet curves around him and smacks harmlessly into a wall. The room is suddenly filled with the telltale dark magic stench of burnt metal and rotting meat.

Rarer still is the human servant who is also a trained black magic adept. This is the only one that I have ever encountered in all of the time I have been a gun.

This is not our lucky day.

CHAPTER THREE

"Might we dispense with any more aggression for the moment? If I wished you dead you would be dead. I merely wish to chat. You can call me Jeremy." His mild voice contains more menace than if he was snarling threats.

"So talk then." My scars are flaring up terribly with him standing there, so much so that I can't tell if it is all because of him or if there are more Renfields out there ready to rush us. I hold both guns pointed at the floor, but that can change in less than a heartbeat. I nod at the girl and she lowers her gun as well.

"Not here. Not unless you wish to explain to the nice officers that you are a member of a secret organization known, unimaginatively enough, as The Order, dedicated to killing older vampires who prey on humans to the point of killing them. By the way young lady, the vampire you maimed is most unhappy with you and is eager to make your acquaintance."

The thing's voice is like finger nails on a chalkboard and makes me want to empty both guns at him. Human servants are difficult to kill, but not impossible, still I need answers and dead mouths don't spew much information.

"Who is your master? What, beyond maybe tearing my throat out, does he or she want with me?" I ask as calmly as I can.

"All in due time dear boy, all in due time. Come with me now. We walk away from here in full light of day and find a place to sit and chat, just the three of us. Won't that be lovely?" The thing's face is impassive and in the distance I can hear the thin wail of sirens.

"After you." I tell him gesturing with my gun for him to go first. That mocking smile flits across his face, but he complies and we move briskly but cautiously through and out of the warehouse.

We walk away from the warehouse, a strange trio indeed. An ex nun, a converted Renfield and something that was more demon than human. Police cars filled the alley leading to the warehouse as we walked away. Another mess left behind. The girl and I have put our guns away for the moment and I am hoping that we won't have to pull them out again.

Together we move down the street to a small spot where a few tables and benches surround a statue of some dead white guy or another. We sit down, Keela by my side and the human servant across from us. He smiles his mocking grin and I grind my teeth to fight the urge to take my chances and empty my gun in his bland yet terrible face.

"I would tell you, dear boy, that what I have to say is for your ears only. However, after the stunt your little friend here pulled last night I doubt Belinda, the vampire she so foolishly maimed, will let her live much past nightfall tonight, so I think we can safely dispense with such considerations." He says giving her a lurid wink.

He is feeding on the fear he is causing her, I can feel that much. Dark magic is based on fear, pain, suffering and death. I want answers, but my patience is running thin.

A woman walks by holding the hand of a little girl, maybe seven years old. She has blonde hair and is dressed in a yellow sundress.

The human servant sucks in his breath and stares hard at the child as he licks his thin lips.

Before I can stop myself my hand flashes out with more than human speed and bitch slaps him so hard that he almost falls out of his chair.

He stands and power absolutely boils around him. Keela curses under her breath and scoots her chair back away from him. I lock eyes with the thing and wait to see what will happen next.

The human mask he was wearing wavers and the dark thing he has been made into glares through for a moment. The smell of scorched metal and rotting meat is almost too strong to bear and he is trembling with the need to attack me.

The glass in the table cracks and the pavement beneath his feet begins to smolder. His fists are clenched and his eyes have emptied of anything human. The hand that slaps him feels unclean and without breaking eye contact, I compose my face into an expression of disgust and slowly and deliberately wipe the hand on my pants.

As quickly as it came the moment of violence passes. He takes a deep shuddering breath and sits back down across from us.

"That will have to be addressed, Joe Gunn also known as Black Irish. It will be addressed most severely indeed at a later time. For now I will do my master's bidding and tell you what I was sent to tell you and then our business will be concluded. But, as I have said, what you just did will be addressed. Oh, so very severely shall it be addressed. Joe Gunn, I know your true name by the way. Part black and part Irish, tell me what parts are Irish?"

"My fists and my liver motherfucker, now tell me why you came and be gone you, you useless shit stain." I put as much disdain into my voice as I could.

He is calm now, my insult slides by him and his mocking smile is back in place. Ignoring the girl he focuses his attention entirely on me.

"I serve Martin."

I keep my face as impassive as his, but his words rock me. Martin is one of the oldest and most reclusive vampires in the region. The Order has never had cause to move against him, because he has long ago evolved beyond the need to kill as he feeds. He and his protégés feed only off animals and willing unglamoured humans, in it for the sexual thrill. Most of the area master vamps pay him homage and leave him and his strictly alone. He sits high up on the vampire council and wields a lot of authority in local vamp affairs.

For all his reputation for good behavior towards humans he is also known to be keenly interested in the dark arts. Vampires can't wield true magic, a limitation that both fascinates and frustrates them greatly. Their glamour powers aren't strictly speaking magic, more an innate ability. Hence the tendency amongst those with such interests to create such creatures as the one sitting across from me. The Order has no proof that he has crossed the line with his dark little hobby, so we have thus far left him alone.

To further complicate matters the last vampire I killed was one of his lieutenants.

Awkward.

"This does not concern your last hunt. Reginald was over two hundred years old, he knew the risks he took by killing those young women. My master would have destroyed him himself for breaking the restrictions he holds all his folk to and for bringing the attentions of your order down on them. You merely saved him the trouble. He wishes to speak to you on an unrelated matter."

"And what might that be?"

The thing actually looks embarrassed for a moment, so fleeting that I might have imagined it. He shifts uncomfortably in his chair and glances away before answering.

"He…has not chosen to share that information with me. He bids me to tell you that he will await your visit tonight, an hour past sunset at his compound. He bids me to inform you that upon his word as an Elder, you will have safe passage, no matter the outcome of your discussion. For tonight you are off limits to any aggression. He bids me to give you his clan ring as a token of this vow."

His pale hand slowly sets a darkly gleaming obsidian ring in front of me. Vamp energies seethe around the thing and without even touching it, I know that it is hundreds of years old. It is indeed the clan ring of an elder vampire.

"Make that invitation for plus one." I grin at him.

"Excuse me?"

"No deal unless the oath covers the girl as well, you do want to come with don't you?" I turn the grin on the girl and she hesitates but then nods her answer.

"That is outrageous." He hisses at me.

"Just part of my boyish charm, the whole outrageous things, I have been told that it can be a bit annoying at times. Oh, and I will pick the hour of both my arrival and my departure. If terms can be met that is. Go running back to your master errand boy and have him contact me by crow if he accepts my terms." I make a shooing motion with both hands.

He glowers at me for a long minute but then gives an eloquent little shrug and stands, picking up the ring as he does so.

"Very well Black Irish, I will be in touch in the usual fashion. A word of caution, check the attitude when you speak to my Master. He is less, forgiving than I am."

"Duly noted shit stain, now be on your way."

Without another word he strolls into a small patch of shadow cast by the statue. The moment he enters the shadow he vanishes.

Yeah, they can travel through shadows. Hate that.

Keela stands up suddenly and runs over to some bushes and begins to throw up violently. The presence of black magic does that to some people. Of course it might be that she just had to kill a couple of people, if you count Renfields as people.

Which for the record I don't.

CHAPTER FOUR

She comes back and sits down at the table, pale and shaky but holding it together.

"You ok?" I ask her softly.

"That….thing is an abomination." She looks ill again and shudders as she answers.

"No argument from me on that girl."

"I can't believe you bitch slapped a demon."

"More of a, low rent demon wanna-be, but yeah that might have been pushing my luck just a bit. You don't really have to come to the meet tonight you know. There is a secure location I can stash you at until The Order can make arrangements to get you safely away from this region. Vamps are territorial, so the odds are good the one you maimed won't leave the region to look you up."

"If someone melted my face off, I might go to the trouble of finding them." She said with a little spunk beginning to trickle back into her voice.

"She will heal, probably already has actually. Come nightfall she will rise, feed and be good as new. Still, you caused her great pain and worse you kept her from following her master's orders. You are likely pretty high up on her hit parade just now."

We sit in silence for a few minutes enjoying the, rare to us Seattle natives, feel of the sun on our skins and relishing the fact that we just narrowly escaped death. Body bags are coming out of the warehouse down the alley, but we aren't in them. For now we will call that a win.

I stand up and she follows me to where I stashed the Harley, lo and behold it is still there. I look it over carefully to make sure nobody has added any nasty surprises. A Renfield once tried to take me out with a car bomb and little experiences like that tend to make one more cautious.

"Where are we going?" She asks as she climbs gracefully onto the bike, watching her long legs swing over the seat stirs ideas in me that I quickly slap down.

Her vows aside, we are in the thick of things now and distractions get you killed in my line of work.

"We are off to see the wizard."

I start the bike and the roar of the engine drowns out any more questions she might have. Motorcycles are great for that. They have ended more than one unwanted conversation between a man and a woman.

As we ride away, I think about what made me slap our nasty little pal Jeremy. It is a trip down memory lane I am not fond of taking, but sometimes our thoughts go where they will.

They take me now back to the last time I faced the vampire that had enslaved me.

I stood before her, my head bowed like a good little slave. Desperate for her glance, her touch, any little crumb of approval or even attention. Desperate to serve her in any way she saw fit to command…..

She had been almost four hundred years old and was past the point that she could pass for human. Her skin was too pale, her eyes shone with an unnatural shine, her features too alien and as with any vamp over two hundred, she was completely hairless. No amount of glamour could possibly make her seem human enough to go out and hunt for herself.

Which is why she needed a Renfield to go out and bring victims to her, which is why she needed me.

"Do you love me?" She had whispered in the darkness. Her voice a collage of seductive echoes.

Of course I did, I loved her more than life itself. I was her total slave, her merest whim my command. It still sickens me to think of it. To think of the things I did in the name of that love.

The things that I am trying even now to pay penance for.

"Tonight I would like a taste of something sweet, loyal one. Something special, a treat if you will. Would you bring me a treat my loyal one?"

A command disguised as a question.

"Bring me a child."

No more tripping down memory lane. I have gotten careless, a glimpse in the rear view mirror shows a beat up blue Econoline van that is obviously following us. They are hanging back, but to my enhanced instincts for such things, they might as well be flying a flag labeled 'Bad Guys r Us.'

A nasty suspicion flashes into my mind, it would explain the blown safe house and the van behind us. A sign shows a rest area coming up and I take the exit to it.

The van slows but doesn't take the exit. They move on ahead. If what I suspect is true, they don't need to follow us too closely.

I park the bike and step off of it. She is looking at me with a mouthful of questions she isn't asking.

"Empty your pockets girl. I think we have been bugged." I take a wand out of the bikes saddle bags that coincidently enough, the man we are on our way to see provided me with, it is designed to detect listening devices and tracking devices.

She tosses the contents of her purse and pockets on the ground in front of me. The wand stays silent so she isn't the problem.

I empty my own pockets and the wand makes angry noise at the box of bullets she brought me.

So then again, maybe she is.

She goes pale and starts shaking her head at me, she is about to protest her innocence when I hold a finger to my lips and shake my head right back at her.

I dump the bullets out on the grass and carefully tear the box apart looking for the bug. When I find it, I remove it carefully and walk over to a bright red new looking pickup truck and toss it into the back.

Confusion to our enemies.

"I swear to you Joe, on all I hold dear that I didn't know." She tells me in a hushed voice as I walk back to her.

I am inclined to believe her. I mull it over as I pick up the bullets and stash them in an inside pocket of my jacket. Priests run widows, they arrange supply drops and such things. Following normal procedure, she likely got a text on this week's talk and toss cheap cell phone, telling her to pick up a package taped underneath a certain pew at a certain church and to bring it to a certain man at a certain location. I remember her telling me about the priest who recruited her and a picture begins to develop.

"Take my hand." I tell her gruffly.

She won't like what is going to happen next. Magic isn't officially recognized by the church of course, but we use it all the same. I have about a dozen or so set spells that I have been taught, I don't understand them, but I don't have to. A baker just needs to follow the recipe to make the cake turn out, he doesn't need to understand why it works. Magic is the same deal, I only need to follow the set spells and rituals I have been taught, I don't need to be an adept to run white magic. The hide me ward I placed on the bike, the spell masking her location to vamps, are good examples of this.

We are about to attempt something a bit more ambitious.

This type of magic is one of the few advantages that humans have over the vamps. We can do magic, and quite simply they can't. They can't wield either white or dark magic, while us human folk can and do wield both.

Tentatively, staring me right in the eye the whole time she reaches out and takes my hand. Like I said, the girl has spunk to spare. I find myself hoping she survives our acquaintanceship. I say the words I have been taught and sketch the rune in the air between us with my free hand.

Instantly the world around us falls away to be replaced by her memory of what happened the day she picked up the bullets to bring to me. I see it all through her eyes through our weird little Vulcan mind meld, yeah I am a Trekkie, get over it.

I see what she saw that day, hear what she heard, feel what she felt. She was nervous, excited and proud to be serving the cause. She entered the church and went straight to where she had been told the package would be and sure enough taped beneath the thirteenth pew on the left hand side of the church, there it was. She slipped it into her purse and looked around before leaving.

That is what I needed to see, that quick look around through her eyes.

There had been a man standing in the shadows glaring at her with a smug expression on his face. She had not consciously registered him, but he was there in this memory trace I was trying to exploit.

A priest whose nose had not so very long ago been broken.

Just as suddenly as the connection between us had been formed, it shattered flinging both of us gasping for air to the ground.

I struggled to my feet first and then helped her up. We stood staring at one another for a moment, this kind of magically enforced intimacy feels like a form of rape on both sides. We were in each other's heads, and I know that what is in my mind amounts to a dirty walk through a bad neighborhood.

Not her though, her soul is cleaner than mine by far, she is who she says she is and can be trusted. She stares at me hard for a moment and then she tells me something so softly, that for a moment I think that I might have imagined it.

"Every saint has a past and every sinner has a future."

"Is that in the bible?" I ask just as softly even though I know the answer.

"No, Oscar Wilde. Liberal Arts major."

We leaned into one another for one warm, delicious moment and then she pulled away.

"What now?" She asks crisply, all business.

I stand apart from her without answering for a moment, dealing with the feelings raging through me before answering.

"Like I said girl. We are off to see the wizard."

Not looking at each other we get back on the bike and thunder out of the rest stop. She is stirring feelings in me that I cannot afford right now. Enough for the moment to know that I can trust her, we are burning daylight and come dark fall we will have our hands full enough without anything else being added to the mix.

Especially as something as complicated as feelings.

CHAPTER FIVE

I park the bike outside of a tan box of a house in an expensive neighborhood near Lake Union.

"We need intel and some supplies. The man who lives here is a Widow, like you. He lost his wife to a vamp attack and was recruited by The Order several years ago. His name is Brian, I call him Brain. You might have heard of him by another name, lots of people call him The Wizard."

She thinks for a minute and then nods. I figured his name would have come up during her training, the guy is something of a legend in the circles we move in.

He is hands down, the best computer guy The Order has.

There has been a lot of talk in the news lately of the Silk Road, the dark secret underbelly of the internet, where you can buy anything from heroin to sex with Peruvian midgets. Well, that dark underbelly has an even darker one beneath it. Vamps came late to the whole internet party, but they are in it in a big way now. Brian has hacked his way into their networks and given us a glimpse into how their world works. A good portion of what we know about vampire politics, culture and methodologies has come from his work. When The Order first instructed him to work with me, he almost quit in disgust and rage.

Brian had loved his wife deeply and completely. He had built a life with her that seemed full of promise, funded by the insane money companies paid as they fell all over themselves to pay him for his skills. Then one hot August afternoon a Renfield had done a snatch and grab while she had been out jogging and delivered her to his master.

The vampire had been young to be using Renfields, barely seventy five. At the time it had been something of a status symbol trendy thing for the younger vamps to have a Renfield or two even though they could still pass for human and do their own hunting.

The Renfield had gotten careless disposing of the body and it had been found. The police had blamed the bloodless mutilated corpse on an unknown serial killer, but one officer who had ties to The Order had known a vampire kill when he saw one. The Order had paid the broken computer genius a visit and had given him a new purpose in life, if they hadn't, he likely would have either blown his brains out or drank himself to death inside of a year.

Then I came along and my handler introduced me and explained what I used to be. That was almost the end of his work for The Order.

I had been instructed to gain his trust and win him over. I succeeded, but did it in my own way.

I went out and found the vamp that had done his wife and instead of killing him myself and therefore losing one of my marks, I bound the little hipster blood sucker in silver chains and delivered him, coincidentally enough on one hot August night, to Brian. Handing him a sawed off shotgun full of priest blessed buckshot, that had been soaked in Holy water, then plated with silver. I had looked him in the eye and told him I would be back for the body.

I had barely walked out of the door when I heard the double boom of him giving the vamp both barrels.

We got along much better after that.

He lets me store a few things here and a couple of them are things I will want for the meeting tonight. I also need to send an encrypted report to The Order bringing them up to date on what has been happening.

"We won't be here long. What is the name of the priest who recruited you? The one whose nose you broke."

She smiles a little at the memory, I really like this girl.

"Father Duncan Larson. Haven't seen him since though."

"He was there when you picked up the ammo. Is that his parish you were in?"

"No, that makes no sense. His church is all the way across town."

Something stinks about this whole mess, the ripe stench of set ups and double crosses and hidden agendas. I would like to have a few answers before night fall and have some idea what we will be walking into.

Brian answers the door before I knock, I know he has cameras scanning every inch of his property, so he knew we were here as soon as we pulled up.

"Password!" He barks pointing a huge stainless steel 357 Magnum revolver at us. Dude is a heavyset, balding guy who looks like he slept in front of his computer last night in the clothes he had been wearing all week. Come to think of it, that's probably exactly what he did do.

I hear Keela suck in her breath and feel her tensing up next to me. Her hand starts to drift towards the gun in her purse.

"Asshole." I tell him calmly.

He lowers the gun and starts laughing as he waves us inside.

"Close enough brother, close enough, come on in and bring your pretty friend with you."

We step into his front room and it looks like the cover of computer nerd monthly. Every conceivable piece of computer related gadgetry covers every level surface. Tech manuals, pizza boxes and empty cans of beer and Red Bull complete the décor.

The guy is such a slob, a brilliant talented slob, but a slob none the less. He is also likely the closest thing my life permits in the way of a friend.

I introduce him and the girl, they are both Widows, for all I know they have a secret club handshake or something. Leaving them to chat for a moment, I sit down in front of the laptop he has dedicated for my use and send my superiors an encoded email bringing them up to speed.

When I come back into the room they are sitting having what smells like decent coffee, I help myself to some and sit down with them.

"Need you to pull a file for me, everything we have on one Father Duncan Larson."

"Won't help you much brother, you won't be talking to him. It's been all over the nets, when he started his car this morning, instead of going vroom vroom it went boom boom." He told me cheerfully.

Yeah he talks like that.

Sounds like someone didn't want to leave any loose ends. This just keeps getting better and better. I can't shake the feeling that I am missing something, some random piece of the puzzle that would make all this weirdness make sense.

The priest was obviously in on setting us up, he somehow knew that the girl would be bringing the package for me and either bugged it or arranged for it to be bugged. Why? No idea. Bribery or blackmail maybe. With him splattered all over his driveway it would be hard to get those answers.

"Ok Brain, I need to gather a few things and borrow a car. Whoever is following us around will be looking for the bike."

"Take the black Jag. Try not to destroy it."

I walk back to a spare bedroom where I keep a weapons locker and open it up. What I want is right on top.

The Order employs an old Chinese man who keeps a shop deep in the heart of the International District, otherwise known as China Town. Old bastard makes the best custom knives out there and the one I am holding now is my personal favorite.

Modified Bowie with a partially serrated edge, eight and half inch blade with a five and half inch hilt, complete with skull crusher pommel. He lined the edge of the blade with a thin coating of blessed silver and the thing is wicked sharp. The hilt is black with silver runes worked into it, all in all a lethal work of beauty. I slide it into a scabbard that I will sling over my shoulder so I will just have to reach behind me to draw it and I set it aside.

I take out the sawed off double barrel that I gave Brain that certain hot August night and set it aside as well. I slip a Snake Slayer .45 Derringer into my leather jackets inside pocket, along with a few extra cartridges and I strap a Smith and Wesson Bodyguard Revolver to my left ankle.

I was never a Boy Scout, but I do believe in being prepared.

She did well with the little Ruger, so I upgrade her to a forty caliber High Point. All the guns are now loaded with the blessed hollow points, so we are good to go.

I hand her the gun as I come back out of the room with the vault and she smiles at me and puts it in her purse.

Brain rummages around in an old beat up filing cabinet and comes out with a small brown bottle with a spray nozzle on top. He grins sarcastically at me as he holds it up.

"You know you want some big boy."

I groan. The older vamps can not only roll you with their eyes using their glamour to take over your will, they can also do dirty tricks with the harmonics of their voices to do the same. Martin is very old and likely very skilled at such games. The Order has a chemist on staff that came up with a compound that grants temporary immunity to this form of assault.

Problem is it stings like hell and smells like a skunk covered in dog shit set on fire with cheap kerosene.

I nod and he feints towards spraying me, but instead gets an unsuspecting Keela square in the face, she goes down making gagging noises, and then it is my turn.

Jesus, the stuff is awful! It burns my eyes and skin on contact and, like I said, the smell is beyond terrible. Just when you think you can't stand it another second, both effects vanish, leaving just a slight tingle on the skin so you know it is working.

I stop her before she can break his nose and explain the necessity of it, she isn't happy, but she doesn't hit him. Even though I am almost inclined to let her, the way the big dope is standing there grinning at us.

"You two should grab a couple hours of sleep. I will wake you up a few minutes before sunset. While you guys crash I will snoop around the vamp nets a bit and see if I can find anything out. There are plenty of bedrooms upstairs, pick one each or share one, up to you crazy kids." He winks at us and sits down in front of one of his countless monitors and begins typing away at the keyboard. In seconds he is totally absorbed in what he is doing and it is like we don't exist.

I snag a beer from his fridge and we say our good nights at the top of the stairs, I watch her walk away and unabashedly enjoy the view. My hopeful male brain tells me that she is putting a little extra sway in her step, because she knows that I am watching. But then I remembered that

58

God hates me and I go to the bedroom I usually use when I crash here.

I drink my beer and I lie down, sleep doesn't come easy to me. On some level I think I fight sleep knowing what dreams will be waiting for me. Most nights I toss and turn, wrestling with my demons moving in and out of various nightmares.

Tonight I know what nightmare awaits me.

My master's voice is the single predominate trait that I will remember about her, a whispered guttural sexy husk that massaged all the pleasure centers in my brain. I used to live for the moments where that voice was focused on me, lived for the opportunity to serve that voice. Disobeying that voice never once even occurred to me.

Until the night that she asked me to bring her a child.

I was already a monster. I had already done things that to this day shame me, things that as I already have mentioned I am spending what remains of my days doing bloody penance for.

She stood there before me in all her glory with the expectation of obedience. What was this last little line to be crossed? I was hers, body and soul, hers to command no matter how foul the deed. A part of my mind was already working on the problem of where to find a child for her, even as another part rebelled against the idea.

"No." I managed to utter, even though it made me want to be violently ill. It made me want to crawl into a dark corner and tear my disobedient tongue out of my own mouth and offer it up to her.

I still remember the utter devastating silence that had fallen between us after that painful utterance. Her stare had sharpened and I had fallen to my knees before the awful weight of it.

"No?" She had hissed and her voice had been like a whip against my skin with salt rubbed into the wounds.

With God as my witness, to this very day, I do not know where I found the strength to struggle to my feet and croak the word out one last time.

"No."

She went absolutely still, in the way that only vampires can. It can't be explained if you haven't seen it. It is more than just the absence of movement, it is more the proverbial calm before the storm sort of thing. I knew that when she did move, it would be to tear my disobedient unworthy throat out.

But then all hell broke loose.

Two Guns burst into the room with submachine guns and emptied their magazines into her. I can still hear her screaming as the bullets tore her apart. She fell to the ground a bloody, twitching mess and then they splashed gasoline on her and set her on fire.

I sat there with my head bowed and waited for one of them to kill me. The younger of the two was ready to oblige, he put a gun to my head and was about to pull the trigger when the older one stopped him.

"This one is mine." Was all he had said.

When I dream about that night, I often dream that I had obeyed my beautiful master and brought her a terrified screaming child. I dream that I handed that child over to her and stood there listening to her feed and waiting for her to tell me what a good little slave I was.

Waking up with a scream in my throat is just another form of penance for the things I have done.

CHAPTER SIX

I walk out of Brain's house and down the street a bit and stop in front of an unfinished condo. I swear these things sprout up like mushrooms overnight. This one seems almost finished. Some lucky yuppies will soon have the starter home of their dreams. The sun is setting and in a few moments it will be full dark.

Reaching into my pocket I pull out a single crow feather, I hold it to my lips and say the right words and then let it go.

Then I wait.

My scars are quiet, so there is no trouble in the immediate vicinity, but my hand is on the gun in my pocket anyway. Opportunity may knock, but it has been my experience that trouble just kicks the damn door in.

A crow silently spirals down to land at my feet. It is holding the same ring Jeremy tried to give me in its beak and it drops it on the ground in front of me.

"Terms accepted. Come to us Black Irish at the hour of your choosing." The crow croaks out the words harshly and then vanishes in a burst of flame and a puff of foul smelling smoke.

I pick up the ring and put it in my pocket. Then I hustle back to the house because apparently the party is on.

Brain is sitting with Keela drinking coffee, she is laughing at some stupid thing he said and the sweet sound of her laughter seems to both wound and heal me at the same time. Not a lot of laughter in my current line of work and death is our retirement plan.

"Party is on girl, we need to pack up and be on our way. You don't have to come you know. This idiot can keep you safe tonight and The Order can help you disappear. " I tell her gruffly.

"In for a penny in for a pound." She says brightly getting to her feet. She kisses Brain on the forehead and walks right past me and out the front door.

"Oh I like her." Brain says shaking his head ruefully at me with a smirk on his face.

"Shut up. You got anything for me?"

"Nope. Don't know what it means, but all of the vamp nets were quiet as the proverbial grave. Also, nothing came through yet from The Order. Watch your back Joe, this is all even weirder than usual. I have programmed the car's GPS system with the address of Martin's compound." He tosses me the keys to the Jag.

I nod at him and head out the door. I hear him engage all the various locks and know that he has activated the assorted nasty surprise booby traps he has on the building and its surroundings. Brain is smart enough to take security very damn seriously. Especially after night fall. You don't serve The Order for as long as he has without a healthy level of paranoia.

Keela waits for me at the car. Both she and the car are things of sleek beauty, but concentrating on her will just buy me trouble. So I go the safe route and give the car a long look.

Jaguar F type, supercharged 3.0 liter V6 with 380 HP at your fingertips. Zero to sixty in just under five seconds, black as night with chrome wheels and other highlights. Brain is a very wealthy guy with really good taste in cars, you forget sometimes because he looks like such a shambling, rumbled train wreck.

This isn't even his nicest car, it is just the nicest car he is willing to let me use. Guy has trust issues.

I swear you total one Colby Mustang in a high speed vampire chase and you never hear the end of it.

"We going to live through this?" She asks me quietly as we get in the car.

"Hell girl, let's go find out." I grin at her as I turn the key and bring that big engine with all that sweet horsepower to life.

I peel out of Brain's driveway leaving serious rubber on the pavement and I can almost hear him cursing me out from behind his locked doors.

You got to take your fun where you can find it.

Out on the road, I take us to the speed limit and leave it there. Not a great idea to get pulled over for speeding when you are a large scary looking black guy who is armed to the tee. If the cops didn't shoot me, The Order would pull strings and eventually get me released, but I haven't got time for that just now.

Keela checks the GPS and we are heading for a rural area near Bothell. We will be there in less than an hour. Assuming we survive the meeting, we will hopefully leave knowing more than we did going in.

"Follow my lead when we get there. Say nothing to anyone, answer no questions, unless I say so. Don't let them goad you into doing something stupid. We are there under truce so they won't start any violence, but if you attack them, they are allowed to defend themselves. You won't survive them doing that." I told her flatly.

She swallows hard and nods at me.

"That nasty crap Brain sprayed you with will give you some resistance to glamour but don't get cocky. Try not to look any of them in the eye and if you feel like they are getting inside your head chant the Lord's Prayer to yourself. We are there to find out what he wants and to hopefully get him to answer some questions, not to go to war."

I can tell she is afraid and that's good. It would be insane not to be afraid under the circumstances, but I can also sense her determination to see this thing through, no matter the cost. Maybe after this is over I will have her tell me what happened with her mother and brother, she will either answer me or try to break my nose, I suppose.

I turn on the CD player and I am suddenly reminded that Brain is my friend. The guy went ahead and loaded up an Elvis CD while I was sleeping.

She gives me a look of total disbelief as The King begins to croon "Blue Moon."

"Seriously?"

"He is called The King for a reason, baby girl. Lean back and enjoy the ride."

I apologize for my love of Elvis Presley to no man, vampire or woman.

So listening to my favorite tunes riding in a sweet car next to a beautiful woman, things could be worse.

Oh yeah, left out the part where we are walking into a compound full of vamps to face their eight hundred year old leader and his semi demonic human servant. That takes some of the fun out of it for sure.

My scars light up like crazy while we are still a half mile out and the telltale sour taste fills my mouth. Christ, there must be a dozen vamps ahead of us and some of them, hell a lot of them, are over a hundred years old. At the center of all of it, I can feel Martin, the oldest of them all. He likely sired many, if not most of the vamps, I am sensing. My arm burns, but I use my training to push the pain to a back corner of my mind. The girl sits next to me oblivious to the dark energies coming from just ahead of us, but she is about to get up close and personal with them.

A few minutes later and we are outside of what is essentially an unmarked, gated community surrounded by a high wall. We are stopped at a checkpoint by two human guards armed with AR-15s and who don't look like they will smile at any of my jokes.

They motion for me to roll down the window and I do. The bigger of the two gives me a hard stare and looks at his smart phone comparing the picture on it to me.

"Did they get my good side? Am I wearing blue, because blue just really makes my eyes pop, you know?" I am giving him shit because to me it is as natural as breathing.

"Go forward up the main drive and park in front of building two. Mister Jeremy will meet you there and escort you to the Master."

I look at him carefully, he is not a Renfield, just a very well paid human mercenary. Interesting.

We do as we have been told and sure enough Jeremy is standing there waiting for us. He is dressed in an immaculately tailored black suit with an expensive looking red silk tie. Before we get out of the car Keela gives me a quick kiss.

"For luck." She tells me.

"You know how this whole scene worked out in Star Wars right? She ends up being his sister."

"Thanks to the vamps, big guy, I am no one's sister. Not anymore." There are tones in her voice of loss and remorse that I don't know what to do with, so I just get out of the car.

I look around, the place is big. Several buildings ranging from what looks like storage sheds to two big four story buildings. Off a little ways I can hear the mooing of cows. They must keep a small herd to provide blood for this many vamps. The willing human donors who live here can only supply so much without dying and if they were dying, The Order would have intervened by now.

Probably by sending me.

"Jerry! What up brother? Having a good night? Read any good dark spell books lately? How's the family?" I gush at him as we get out of the car.

Sarcasm is just one of the many services I offer.

"Good evening to you as well, Black Irish. Nice to see you again Keela, I see you are still foolish enough to keep such very bad company. Oh well, that will work out as it will I suppose. Shall we get on with it then?" His sickly sweet voice hasn't improved since we last met. Not good news that he knows Keela by name now, but not unexpected either.

Suddenly there are seven vampires, all over a hundred years old standing behind Jeremy. Never saw the barest hint of movement, but here they are. Three woman and four men, all dressed just as formally as the human servant. All of them with unreadable faces staring at us without blinking.

I hate it when they do that.

"What are they for, Jerry?" I ask him mildly.

"Consider it an honor guard of sorts, as well as a compromise. You may keep all your silly little guns as long as they can act as a buffer between you and our master. Have no fear, it will not be us that breaks this truce. On that you already have my master's vow."

"Fair enough, lead on, oh royal errand boy and all around lapdog. Let's go see what your master has on his very ancient and no doubt totally bat shit crazy mind." Yeah I know, I told Keela not to respond to goading and to start no trouble.

Do as I say not as I do.

He gives me a long look that suggests he would recommend I not buy any unripe bananas because of the odds of my surviving long enough to eat them are so poor. But then he gives a small shrug and leads us to the door of building two. He opens it, walks in and the seven vamps form up around us and together we all move this show indoors.

CHAPTER SEVEN

A human string quartet plays softly in one corner of the room as we walk in. There are no electric lights on, but dozens of candles burn on velvet draped tables, all over the place. Vampires are fucking everywhere.

I count twenty and stop counting. They are of every size, gender and race I can think of. No newbies, the youngest one I can sense is at least seventy five. It is all very, civilized. They are all drinking blood out of crystal goblets and apparently enjoying the music.

The quartet isn't Elvis, but they aren't bad.

Nobody pays us any attention as Jeremy and the seven vampire dwarves lead us up a long red carpet leading up to a dais with a long black leather couch on it.

Martin's age and power is a weight I can feel on my soul. Being around this many powerful vampires is pulling at the vampire taint in me, bringing it out. I know that if I were to look at Keela right now she would be startled by my eyes, which have likely gone all vamp. Solid black with no whites at all. Once again I fall back on my training to keep that part of me in check and after a few moments I am solidly in control again.

He sits on the couch, sucking gently at a bite on the wrist of the naked young woman sitting next to him. She is supermodel beautiful, her eyes closed and head thrown back in the bliss of being fed upon.

Yeah, it feels that good. Right up to the point that you die, that is.

He is bald of course, as are all of the ancients. No eyebrows either. His face is a study in razor sharp angles, high cheekbones and a sharply pointed nose and chin. He is tall, willowy and pale beyond imagining. He looks up at us and softly pushes the woman away. Two Asian female vamps come and help her walk shakily away to disappear behind some curtains at the back of the room.

Jeremy walks up and bows low before him. Martin touches him on the shoulder and motions for him to sit beside him. In the blink of an eye, the seven vamps are standing behind the couch.

"The Legendary Black Irish, welcome to my humble home good sir. Welcome also to you Ms. Keela. Come forward then and let us begin our business." His voice is hushed and calm and I know that without the crap that Brain sprayed us, it would be lulling us into a false sense of security. I look over at the girl and so far she seems ok, her hands are clenched tightly at her sides, but she hasn't freaked out just yet.

We take a few steps closer, I can feel his stare on me. The quartet has changed its tune now. All at once they begin playing an instrumental version of the old Elvis song "Hound Dog."

"I understand that you are a big fan, Black Irish. Can't say I see the attraction, but then again I suppose that I am hopelessly old fashion."

"Could we maybe cut the crap and get down to business?" I suggest. My nerves are strung tight dealing with the closeness of this many vamps and I am in no mood for cute little games.

If he is offended, he doesn't show it, he merely nods and claps his hands once.

Just like that the room is empty except for us and the quartet which has now stopped playing and simply sits with their hands in their laps looking down at the floor. Oh, and the honor guard standing behind the Master of course. Keela swears softly under her breath at how fast a room full of vamps can move when told to.

Jeremy stands and makes a shooing motion with his hands at the musicians and they stand and take their leave as well. He sits back down and smiles at me.

The smile makes me feel unclean and I resist the urge to put a fist or a clip full of bullets through it.

"Very well Black Irish. We shall dispense with the usual required courtesies and get, as you say, down to business. It is fairly straight forward. You do something for me and I do something for you."

"I am listening." I tell him through gritted teeth.

"An associate of mine has a certain artifact that I require for reasons that frankly do not concern you. I want you to work with Jeremy here to retrieve it and kill her in the process. She has been a very naughty vampire and I do believe that she is on your organizations kill list. It would remove one of those marks that you bear so very stoically." His tone is casual, almost bored.

Can this really be what he wants? It seems unlikely, if he knows anything about how The Order works, he knows that I don't pick my own targets. They are chosen for me and assigned to me by those above me.

"It doesn't work that way." I tell him flatly.

"But it could, could it not? Do this for me and you lose a mark. To sweeten the deal, I will provide you with information that will allow you

79

to track down and put down eight other rather naughty vampires, thus ending your service. It seems a slam dunk, win win scenario to me. I have the list right here with me, like your Santa Claus, I have even checked it twice. I know full well who has been naughty and who has been nice." His tone is playful now, playful in the way that a not very hungry cat might play with a mouse.

Something is going on here, but I will be damned if I know what it is. Some bigger game is being played. This is like trying to put a puzzle together in the dark with a gun to your head and a timer ticking in the background.

"Going to have to pass." I tell him. The next few seconds will tell all. In the face of my refusal will he honor the truce or have us torn apart, piece by bloody piece? My hands are in my pockets on my guns but if it comes to that, we might take a few with us, but we will die.

There is a long drawn out moment where it could easily go either way. Power builds up in the room and the candles suddenly flare brightly. A dark nimbus forms briefly around Jeremy and then flickers out.

"Very well then, Black Irish. I am of course disappointed. Merely speak Jeremy's name while standing in a shadow if you reconsider. You and your lovely companion are free to go." His tone now is bored and dismissive.

"Really? You sent a team of Renfields to be wiped out by me and a vampire who ended up with a face full of Holy water to set this up and now we just walk away?" I ask him

His laughter is one of the most awful sounds that I have ever heard and I feel the girl next to me shudder at the terribleness of it.

"Oh, you humans. Always so very ready to jump to conclusions. I have no Renfields, I have no need of them. Jeremy here merely followed them in to have his little chat with you. Also, and perhaps more importantly the vampire Belinda is no creature of mine. You are both tap dancing blindfolded in a minefield I am afraid. Despite your reputation I do not think that you will prevail in this matter Black Irish.

Take your leave of us now, we have other matters to attend to this night."

Crap. I have been a fool and we are in mortal danger because of it. Time to go. My goal now is to get the girl and I back to Brain's and lock us in for the night, because another team is in this game and they are under no truce with us.

Worse, we have no idea who or what they are.

I nod at them and take Keela by the hand. We turn and start for the door. Each step towards it feels like it could be our last and it seems to take decades to make it to the door. The Master vampire and his human servant seem to ignore us as we leave.

Finally we are in the car and headed out. I hold a finger to my lips as Keela begins to sputter questions at me. No time for such things now, we need to get the hell away from this place.

"Get your guns out and be ready girl. We are in trouble." I snap at her as we race down the road.

She swears like a drunk Marine under her breath, but in a flash both guns are out. The forty caliber is in her hand and the Ruger 9mm is on the seat beside her.

We are almost five miles away before the attack hits.

CHAPTER EIGHT

The vampire Belinda simply appears on the road in front of us. We are doing eighty when we hit her and the car crumbles around her. Both airbags go off and we sit there stunned for a moment.

There is a rending shrieking noise as the passenger door on Keela's side is torn off of its hinges. She screams once and is gone into the night.

I hurt in a lot of places but screw that, there is no time. I draw my High Point and stumble out of the car.

Belinda effortlessly holds Keela by the throat high over her head. She smiles at me as I come towards her.

"As I was telling you Black Irish, before we were so rudely interrupted, my master would like a word with you."

I point the gun at her and walk as close as I dare. I can tell Keela can't breathe and the clock is ticking to save her life.

"Put her down and we will talk." I snarl at her. If I fire it might just piss her off enough to snap the girl's neck like a twig.

"Oh, I don't think so. This one is mine no matter what arrangement you and my Master come to. I will kill her and then I will drag you by the hair you don't have to my master kicking and screaming. Tell me Black Irish, what do you think of that plan?"

I smile at her.

This serves to piss her off.

"You smile, human filth? Should I dispense with all games and just snap the bitch's neck now? Tell me big bad vampire hunter, why do you smile?" She growls at me as she gives Keela a little shake.

"I am smiling vampire bitch, because right this very minute you have a bright red dot in the exact center of your forehead." I tell her calmly.

The shot takes her straight to the head and she reels backwards dropping the girl as she goes. I empty my gun into her and toss it away as I rip my knife from its shoulder sheath.

She is standing up before my blade even clears leather. Snarling, she launches herself at me and I swing the knife as hard and fast as I can.

I damn near take her head off. The blade catches on her spine and she goes down spraying blood and using both hands to try and stem the flow.

And then she gets up again and is coming at me.

Instinctively, I lash out with a roundhouse kick that catches her on the side of her face and completes the job of taking her head off. It rolls over to where Keela lies, trying to catch her breath. She empties the High Point into the head reducing it to pulp.

86

I bury the blade to the hilt in her chest, where the heart should be and twist the blade viciously and she suddenly goes from being a hundred year old pissed off dangerous vamp to being rotting meat.

I sit down suddenly, the wear and tear of the night getting to me. I put my head between my knees and breathe deeply.

"You ok?" I call out, when I have the breath to do so. Little black dots swim in my vision and if I wasn't so damn tough, I might throw up or pass out.

She sits back down and gives me a feeble wave.

The car is totaled, the front end caved completely in and the passenger door is just plain gone. Brain is going to be so pissed at me. That is two cars I owe him now.

Three figures walk out of the woods towards us, two of them are mercenaries from Martin's compound and I know the third.

The man who trained and more or less created me, the man who spared my life the night my master died and brought me into The Order. He comes limping up to us leaning heavily on a black cane, he has a Ruger Mini 14 complete with a Red Dot Laser scope mounted on it slung over his shoulder.

Michael Gunn, ladies and gentlemen, the man, the legend. One of the most successful and infamous Guns of all time.

He shouldn't be here, it makes no sense. The Order retired him over year ago, due to failing health. At best he rides a desk now, not going out on active field missions. Yet here he is with mercenaries in tow, yet another baffling puzzle piece in the fucked up jigsaw that life has been for a couple of days now. He looks like crap, his face is lined and his pony tail is even grayer than the last time I saw him. He is wearing a long black trench coat that looks huge on his wasted away frame.

"I am getting too old for this shit!" He barks at me as he hobbles up to me.

I can't help it, I start laughing when he says this. He ripped off the line from a series of bad movies starring some equally bad actors, but he makes it funny every damn time he uses it!

"What the hell Mike? I mean I appreciate the assistance and all, but maybe you want to tell a brother what the fuck is going on?"

Then the two mercenaries fan out and bring their weapons up to bear on us in a way that makes me uncomfortable. Mike is still hobbling towards me with a fixed grin on his face and suddenly I am not so happy to see him anymore.

He is still grinning as he takes the last couple steps and jam the cane into my chest.

"Treachery and betrayal Lad, treachery and betrayal."

I go to my knees, Christ it hurts. I struggle to rise and he zaps me again. I grunt and fall back down again. From roughly a million miles away I can hear Keela screaming and it gives me the strength to try to rise again. He zaps me a third time and I fall to the cold hard ground, twitching.

I managed to raise my head and make eye contact with him, asking him a silent "Why?" He stares back down at me without a hint of mercy in his dark eyes, no trace of apology or remorse. A thousand questions racing through my mind and I struggle to form the words to just one of them.

Then he clubs me in the head with the cane and all the damn lights go out.

When they come on again, I am zip tied to a chair that is anchored into the concrete floor. Jeremy is sitting across a long table from me grinning like the proverbial cat and canary situation. I have no idea if hours or minutes have passed.

"Ah, Black Irish. You have rejoined us. I was beginning to fear your erstwhile friend and mentor had perhaps hit you just a little too hard. Welcome now to the first day of the rest of your life." His sweetly sick sing song voice had a note of smug anger in it that does not bode well for me enjoying that which is to come.

"Fuck you." Not especially witty, but the best I could do under the circumstances.

"Get out." Michael says as he walks into the room. Jeremy doesn't like it much but he obeys.

Interesting.

My mentor sits down across from me and settles into his chair like every single motion of doing so pains him. He takes a vial of pills from a vest pocket and slips a couple into his mouth. Closing his eyes he leans back into his chair for a moment paying me no attention.

"You swore vows." I croaked at him, my throat dry, making it painful to speak.

He makes a derisive snorting noise and slams his fist down on the table between us.

"Oh yeah, vows to the sacred Order. Let me tell you boy, at one time I was a believer, I truly was. I served a most righteous cause for the glory of God. Then I found out that our most sacred Order had been corrupted. Know what we are now Lad? We take out the trash for the vampire council. That is all. They provide us with the names of the killer vamps and we spare them the embarrassment and inconvenience of cleaning up their own mess. All in the name of God and Country of course. Money, and certain other favors changes hands and business gets done."

I glare at him and force him to follow my eyes as I glance at the scars on my arm and all that they represent.

"Oh yeah Lad, those. Do you know you are the only Renfield in history of such things to be turned away from their master and made into a Gun? Oh, we have tried again, but the subjects have had the uniform habit of just plain dying. We had your master's lair wired for sound and video days before we struck and I have to tell you that you are the only Renfield on record who has ever defied their master and lived. The strength of will you showed by refusing to bring her a child is one factor of that."

He pauses to catch his breath and hacks up something that looks like blood into a handkerchief. Under the circumstances I can't seem to drum up much sympathy for him.

"If not for me my boy, you would have died that night. I saw something special in you, I knew you were destined for something and now I know what."

I flex my hands and know instantly that I will not be able to bust free. Mike knows what he is doing and will not have left me any slack.

"I had your DNA run through The Order data base and found some intriguing things. Through your mother's side of the family you are descendent from a long line of Irish witches, going back to the era of the Druids even. Your father had a few oddities in the family tree as well Boy, so you were suited to the use of magic from birth. Not only did you survive what we did to you with the marks, but you can wield magic. Simple spells to be sure, but with your vampire taint, you should not even be able to do that."

That had never occurred to me. I suppose I thought the taint too small to interfere with the use of magic, but he had a point. Any trace of vampire should have prevented that. I really didn't like where I thought this train of thought was going.

"We were under truce with Martin, he broke his sworn vow." I threw it out there to stall, but I pretty much had already worked that part out.

"No Boy, he didn't. You left his place safe and sound, did you not? You got yourself involved in vamp politics, Martin has his plans for you and Belinda's master, a master vamp named Alicia doesn't want those plans to succeed. Belinda attacked you and the girl, and the mercenaries, I personally hired, collected you. You haven't asked about the girl by the way." He said casually.

I hadn't because I didn't want to dwell on the idea of her dead by the side of the road with a bullet in her head. I looked him in the eye and did my best to silently spell out his death warrant to him.

He laughed, admittedly not the response I was really shooting for. Hard to pull off when you are zip tied to a chair with no hope of escape but hell, I gave it the old college try.

"You are a pisser Lad, you always were. We didn't kill her, she is a feisty one by the way. She tried to kick one of my men in the head. She has a lot of spunk, but spunk don't cut it against armed, trained men. She got a rifle butt to the head and is currently locked up … well, elsewhere. Her fate will be decided later. Let us get back to yours, shall we?"

He stops and coughs some more, it sounds like pieces he still needs inside of him are coming up. I had known he was sick, but I hadn't known it was this bad. Our relationship had always been complicated, sure, he hadn't killed me when he could of, but he had beaten the ruthless training into me, scarred me with an arcane ritual and set me on the path of deadly penance I had been walking for years now.

Hallmark doesn't make a card for that.

CHAPTER NINE

"Jeremy found some reference to a ritual in an ancient text that he thinks he can adapt and combine with the rituals we used to create you. Martin will turn you into a vampire, he will be your sire and you will of course be loyal to him. We are all hoping that you will be the first vampire ever to be able to wield magic. Imagine it Joe, all the strength, speed and power of being a vamp and the dark magic at your call. Jeremy will initiate you and train you in the dark arts. Martin will rise to power on the vampire council by accomplishing this."

No good news for me in any of that. My old master had often spoken of rewarding my services to her by turning me, at one time I had hungered for that very thing. Now I would claw my own throat out and die before I let that happen.

Regrettably that brought us back to the whole zip tied to the chair and helpless thing.

"And what do you get you lying scumbag?"

"I get to live Joe, I have only a couple months to live. Cancer started in my lungs and is just every damn where now. Jeremy will also train me in the dark arts and I will use every sacrificial spell I have in order to cure myself. When I have learned enough to be useful, Martin will make me into another human servant for his entourage and I will live forever. So will you, think of it Boy? You will be the first of a new kind of vampire. Martin thinks that it will tip the balance of power to the point where vampires will rule the world. It is your destiny Lad, accept it!"

He gets up to leave leaning heavily on the damn cane he used to zap me and club me with. If I could get my hands on it right now, I would cheerfully beat his old ass to death with it.

"Next time we meet Joe, you will be a vampire. Martin has assured me that as your master he will not allow you to harm me even if you still wish to. A new age is dawning Boy, and you and I will be on the winning side. You can thank me later."

With that he leaves me.

I can feel the burn marks from the Taser and my head throbs from being clubbed with the cane, but all these injuries are minor. My training forces me to review all of my options which doesn't take me long, because I don't have any.

Jeremy walks back in and walks up to me. He stands over me for a moment as if he is considering his options. Dark magic is rippling off of him in waves and he is almost too distracted by it to care about me.

Almost.

He hauls back and slaps me cross the face so hard that once again for a moment or two the lights go out.

"That evens things up between us Black Irish. When we meet again it will be as fellow adepts. I have so much to show you." The filthiness of his voice makes me want to bathe in Holy Water.

He cocks his head to one side, looking like a dog responding to a whistle that only it can hear. A dreamy look flickers across his bland face and he stands silently for a moment.

"The time approaches and there is much to be done." He tells me patting my head.

And then he is gone.

I have no idea how much time I have before the fun is supposed to start. My head is reeling from the things that Mike told me, the corruption of The Order and the stuff about my parents. My mom had been an Irish American school teacher and my dad a black cop from New Orleans, they both died in a car accident a few days after my twenty second birthday. Hard to imagine a history of magic in my family tree, but it sure would explain some things.

Keela, according to Mike was alive. For the moment I would count that as a win. I allowed myself a quick smile at the idea of her trying to kick the mercenaries' head off of his shoulders, but the smile fades quickly in the face of the trouble that we both are in.

I can't bust the zip ties with brute strength and the chair is bolted down, that leaves me to consider other skills. Magic. I do a mental inventory of the simple spells that I have been taught trying to think of something useful.

Nothing, at least nothing that I have been taught.

That finally leaves one last resort.

Prayer.

Something that I have little experience with, I am afraid.

I went to church as a boy with my parents, but drifted away from it in my teenage years. Then after my parents died senselessly at the hands of a drunk driver, I had even less use for it. I dove into a hedonistic pleasure driven life that I was pretty sure if there was a God, he, she or it would not approve of.

Then I became a Renfield and my new Master became the thing I worshipped above all other things.

Now I am a Gun and have spent the last years of my life trying to do my penance for the sins I have committed. Truth be told, with the stains on my soul, I have not felt clean enough to speak to God through prayer. I have not felt worthy to ask anything of God beyond the chance I was being given to make amends. Corrupt now or not, The Order had given me that chance and like I said it felt like more than I deserved.

But I pray now. I pray for the plans of these monsters to fail, I pray for the safety of Keela and I pray for The Order to prevail in this and to find its way back to righteousness if it has indeed strayed from that path.

I say no prayer for myself, I have already been shown more mercy than I have earned the right to.

The heavens did not part, no beam of light came down to sever my bindings or smite my enemies. I was still secured to a chair, bolted to the floor of an ancient vampire's lair. Nothing had really changed.

Except that a feeling of peace slowly settled down upon me. They would be coming for me soon and if the slimmest chance was presented, I intended to escape and show these bastards my own personal version of The Lord's Prayer.

"Yeah, though I walk through the valley of the shadows, I shall fear no motherfucking evil, because I am the worst God damned thing in the fucking valley to piss off."

I said out loud to the empty room and felt just a little bit better.

CHAPTER TEN

They came for me a little while later. Jeremy, Mike and Martin came into the room and surrounded me. The Master Vampire snaps his fingers and suddenly there are two more vamps in the room with us. He gestures impatiently at me and the chair, and the vamps simply rip the chair free and carry me out of the room. They look so much alike that they could be twins and I immediately name them Bert and Ernie.

Little trip down memory lane, Mike is wearing the same white robes he wore when he sent me down the path of being a Gun. He walks behind us chanting softly as he walks and sketching runes in the air with one withered hand.

Jeremy is also in robes, although his are black and he too is sketching runes into the air and he is using what bears an uncomfortable resemblance to a human arm bone.

A child's arm bone.

Martin leads our dark parade and the Bert and Ernie vampires carry me like slaves used to carry kings. Only they aren't the slaves here, that role has been assigned to me.

They carry me into the same chamber where Keela and I first faced the Elder. All the tables are gone and reaching out with my senses, the only vampires I can feel are the three with us. He must have sent them all away for the night, he must not have wanted any witnesses to what he was attempting. If the ritual fails, they bury the rest what's left of me and no one is the wiser. No harm to his reputation.

If he succeeds, he will make use of the information when he is ready and not before it.

My marks burn as the chanting intensifies, the feeling begins to spread throughout my body. My vision begins to dim and a discordant humming noise fills my ears. The now familiar stench of dark magic begins to become overpowering.

A ring of salt has been poured around the pentagram that has been etched onto the floor. Bert and Ernie set me down in the exact center of it and bowing to their master, retreat to the sidelines.

Martin stands before me now, power coming off of him in waves. He smiles benevolently down at me.

"You will be my most favored of progeny Black Irish. Together we will remake this world."

"You should really come up with an evil laugh if you are going to toss off lame dialogue like that." I tell him snidely.

His hand flashes out and tears my shirt off. He holds a finger up and as I watch the nail on it lengthens and hardens into a razor sharp claw. Using it he carves a single rune into the center of my chest. I suck in my breath at the pain of it and that gets me another calm benevolent smile.

He scratches his own arm and a spray of vampire blood hits me in the face. Once I would have lapped it up like a nectar of the Gods, but now it disgusts me and my arms strain with the effort of trying to tear my hands free so I can wipe it away. The smell and taste of it fills my senses and I begin to gag. The chanting has reached a crescendo and the air in the room thrums with arcane powers.

And then the sweet, sweet sound of fully automated weapons fire begins to fill the room.

The Order has a team of Guns that is our ace in the hole for when the shit really hits the fan. They make the Navy Seals seem like freaking Boy Scouts in comparison and they are here. They are called The Intervention and they are here doing their thing. No idea how or why, but the Calvary has arrived.

Martin twitches as the bullets tear into him and then he bursts into white hot flames as several full clips of incendiary white phosphorus tipped blessed bullets riddle him. He goes down screaming.

Bert and Ernie get the same treatment before they have a chance to use vampire speed to escape and Mike goes down in mid chant falling to the floor in a bloody smoking ruin.

He would have lived longer and died cleaner if he would have waited for the cancer to do its ugly work. Fuck him!

"You owe me another car asshole!" Brain tells me with a savage grin as he cuts me loose with a ridiculous mail order huge survival knife.

"Pretty sure I owe you more than that brother! What the hell is going on?" I gasp as he helps me up.

"I had you take the Jag, because I had it rigged with cameras. I saw Michael Gunn take you down and relayed that info to The Order. They had their suspicions about him anyway. Also, in case you fucked up my car, I wanted to be able to find you. So, I slapped a combination tracker, listening device on your coat while you were sleeping. We heard the whole nasty plan." Brain hands me a pistol from a holster on his hip.

"Bad guy in black robe limped off that way!" He pointed as he turned away to pump more bullets into the twitching form of the Master vampire who was even now struggling to rise to his feet.

Eight hundred year old vampires are not easy to kill, but I leave them to it and follow Jeremy.

He must be in bad shape, human servants don't typically survive the deaths of their masters, but he seems stronger than most and being a dark art adept gives him better odds. I am not following him for vengeance, though I wouldn't mind some.

I am following him hoping that he will lead me to Keela.

The ritual was interrupted, so I was not turned, but something was done, I can feel it. The rune on my chest burns and the marks on my arm now hum with some form of power. There is no time to wonder about it now.

I am catching up to him now, he is slowing as behind us his master begins to die.

He ducks into a room and reemerges holding Keela in front of him like a shield. Her hands are bound behind her and her mouth is covered with duct tape.

"Stay back Black Irish. I have nothing to lose by killing her." He warns unsteadily.

"You don't look so good Jerry, what's up? Feeling a little peaked now that your master is back there doing a pretty darn good impression of a toasted marshmallow?"

Yeah, I know. I just barely survived a demonic ritual and I am still a smartass. It is as much a part of me as whatever weird crap my witchy relatives passed down to me.

"I will survive." He tells me flatly.

"Maybe so, tell you what Jerry, let's play, Let's Make a Deal, OK? You let her go and step into a shadow and do your disappearing act and I will give you a couple day head start before I come for you." I stand still and tuck the pistol in my waist band as I spread my hands out wide.

He seems to consider the offer for a long moment, but then shakes his head ruefully.

"Fuck you!" Then he moves with amazing speed slamming Keela's head into the stone column they are standing by and then picking her up bodily and throwing her aside. She smashes into a wall, slides down it and lies there as limp as a rag doll.

Then he lurches unsteadily towards a shadow.

"NO!" I scream and my voice isn't human. It reverberates with power and rage. The rage fills me and I move faster than I have ever moved before.

He smiles at me mockingly as he steps into the shadow and is gone, but I don't stop moving. Instead I do the impossible.

The arm with my marks seems to move of its own volition and it reaches into the shadow after him. It feels impossibly cold and it's like reaching into a vat of congealed blood, but my fingers get a grip on something and I pull as hard as I can.

I toss him onto the floor before me and he is looking up at me in total shock.

"It isn't possible." He gasps.

Reaching down I haul him to his feet. Holding him by the throat with my unmarked hand, I draw my other hand back.

"Neither is this Mother Fucker! Enjoy Hell!" I snarl at him.

Then I smash my fist into his chest and rip his still beating heart out of his body. I squeeze it into pulp in front of his dying eyes and toss the carcass aside. It lands with a thud several feet away.

I go to Keela and take the tape from her mouth as gently as I can. Without knowing how I do it, I just touch her wrists and the ropes untie themselves and fall away.

A new talent, mind you that would have been handy say, an hour or so ago.

She is breathing, but she is in bad shape. Blood is coming from her nose and ears and one arm is bent at an unnatural angle. Her eyes flutter open and she gives me a smile so weak that it breaks my heart.

"Joe?" Her voice is a bare wounded echo of her usual voice.

"I'm here girl. I am here. I got you. It is all over, Brain came with a strike team and saved the day. Martin is dead, Jeremy is dead, and my former mentor turned asshole traitor, well you guessed it, he is dead as well." I babble as I hold her in my arms.

Down the hallway we hear a final barrage of automatic weapon fire and what is left of Jeremy burst into flame and is gone leaving nothing but a greasy stain.

One of the marks on my arm flares brightly and then fades away to nothingness. Another debt paid. Apparently who or whatever keeps track of such things has put Martin's demise into the win category for me even though I didn't actually literally cause his death.

"Joe, about that whole vow of celibacy thing...." Her voice weak as it was, fading now, dwindling away with the blood flowing from her.

Brain is coming at a full run down the hallway towards us with a medic kit. To my senses he is moving in terrifying slow motion and I wave him to move faster.

"Shush now girl, don't try to talk. Rest, we have got you. You are going to be OK. Stay with me Keela, please stay with me!"

"If I live, about that vow…." Her eyes flutter and she starts to gasp for air.

"Keela!" I shout and see Brain flinch and some of the plaster on the walls around us cracks and falls to the floor.

"If I live….." and she trembles violently once and then goes still in my arms. Her eyes close and her breath stops.

Brain shoves me aside somehow and starts working on her. The other Guns show up and surround us with drawn weapons in case some new threat presents itself, but the party is over. The marks on my arm are quiet and still. They still thrum with the new energies that only time will tell the meaning of.

I sit with my back to the wall and my head in my hands.

The world spins around me, so much has happened in the last couple days that my tired brain cannot seem to process all of it. Bottom line is, that I live to fight another day.

Keela may not.

More proof, if any was needed, that God hates me.

Epilogue-

Three days pass.

Three days of sitting by Keela's hospital bed, waiting to hear if she will live or die.

I have not left her side.

Brain is here as well, and he has somehow smoothed things over with the hospital staff about the big scary black man who will not leave the girl's hospital room. The nurses go about their business and more or less ignore me now.

Maybe he offered to buy them a new CAT scan machine or something. I don't know and don't care what he did, as long as it worked.

The Order did the usual clean up, their spin doctors working overtime to make the story go away. Keela's injuries were blamed on a car accident. Apparently, we hit a really fucking big deer.

It had been a very close thing. Her skull had been fractured, her arm broken and numerous other varied injuries, including internal bleeding. Three surgeries and two flat lines later and I was still sitting by her bedside.

Brain and I have talked about what happened. Both of us were rocked by Mike's disclosure that the Order had become corrupt, for different reasons the organization had become the focus of our lives and it hurt badly that maybe it wasn't what it had been. He is using his skills to check into it. For the time being, I am still a Gun and he is still a Widow.

What we haven't really talked about is what happened to me during the incomplete ritual. We both know I am different now, but we don't know just how deep the differences go. Time will tell.

Martin's vamps have scattered, their master is dead and so now they are free. If they behave themselves, we will leave them alone, if they don't, we will kill them.

Brain says the vamp nets have been all abuzz with various accounts of what happened the other night. Like the commonplace internet, none of it is especially accurate. He says my legend has grown, no matter how true to life the accounts may be.

He also says that I am never borrowing one of his cars again.

So for now, I sit holding Keela's hand and listening to the beeps and pings of the various machines that she is hooked up to. One of her doctors came in just a bit ago and told me that she will live.

He was mildly startled when I hugged him and kissed him full on the lips.

I remember when I was a young child, my mother would sing me songs in Gallic. It is such a beautiful language made for declarations of love, poetry and lullabies. She would sing me to sleep and I swear my dreams would be sweeter for the sound of her voice.

So, now I sit and hold my girls hand. I am alive. She is alive. What is damaged in both of us will heal. I remember what she told me, every saint has a past and every sinner has a future.

I hold her hand and I begin to sing my girl an Irish Lullaby and I start to think that maybe, just maybe.......

God doesn't hate me after all.

THE END

A major portion of this book was written at the Pickled Onion Pub in the Renton Highlands, thanks to the owners and staff there. "Mind Your Pints!" Thanks for the good brew and food!

SNEAK PREVIEW!

IRISH LULLABY

BOOK TWO OF THE BLACK IRISH CHRONICLES

CHAPTER ONE

It is raining again. I have always wondered about something, I have read that the Eskimos have over two hundred words for snow in their language, a different word for every different kind of snow imaginable. It rains so much here in Seattle that you would think we would have our own version of that.

But no, here rain is just rain.

My marks are quiet, no Renfields or vamps anywhere near. I am waiting at an Irish pub near Belltown for Brain and Keela to join me for dinner. I am not expecting any trouble, but there is a loaded High Point 9mm in a holster in the small of my back because, as I have mentioned in the past,

"Opportunity knocks, but trouble just kicks the damn door in."

That was taught to me by my former mentor and trainer, who a few months ago turned traitor and tried to transform me into a vampire who could wield dark magic.

People wonder why I have trust issues.

Brain and Keela have become friends, hell, until her and I find our own place, we are all roommates. Not as awkward as it sounds because his place is so huge.

The waitress who showed me to the table was a knockout and she gave me all the usual signals that my attentions would be most welcome.

I am a one woman man now.

Keela bears a few scars from what happened, physical and otherwise. Hell, so do I for that matter, our bond goes pretty damn deep now. We are happy in a cautious sort of way. Both of us know how fragile our particular existence is. The Order so far has left us alone, a honeymoon period if you will.

A raven taps on the glass window just outside my booth and stares at me with beady little eyes.

Honey moon over.

49R00067

Made in the USA
Columbia, SC
22 January 2018